Graveyard Diaries

APPROACHING THE UNDEAD

magic wagon

by Baron Specter
illustrated by Setch Kneupper

visit us at www.abdopublishing.com

Printed in the United States of America, North Mankato, Minnesota.
052012
092012

This book contains at least 10% recycled materials.

Text by Baron Specter
Illustrations by Setch Kneupper
Edited by Stephanie Hedlund and Rochelle Baltzer
Interior layout and design by Neil Klinepier
Cover design by Neil Klinepier

Library of Congress Cataloging-in-Publication Data

Specter, Baron, 1957-
  Approaching the undead / by Baron Specter ; illustrated by Setch Kneupper.
    p. cm. -- (Graveyard diaries ; bk 2)
  Summary: Stan Summer has been attacked by mysterious balls of light in Hilltop Cemetery and he and his new friend Amy need to solve the mystery of who these ghosts are and what they want.
  ISBN 978-1-61641-899-1
  1. Ghost stories. 2. Haunted cemeteries--Juvenile fiction. [1. Ghosts--Fiction. 2. Haunted places--Fiction. 3. Cemeteries--Fiction. 4. Mystery and detective stories.] I. Kneupper, Setch, ill. II. Title.
  PZ7.S741314App 2012
  813.6--dc23
                                        2011052034

CONTENTS

Chapter 1:
A Gripping Fog

S tan Summer wasn't sure what he was seeing. The evening was dark. The moon was not up, but a red glow was coming from somewhere in the cemetery.

Very odd, he thought. He left his skateboard on the back steps of his house. Then he walked toward Hilltop Cemetery. It began at the edge of his yard.

Stan checked his pockets. He had a pen and his notepad, a flashlight, and half of a candy bar.

He swept the beam of light across the dark yard. Then he shut it off and began to walk.

As he entered the cemetery, he stopped. The red glow was coming from the other side of the hill. Was it a fire? He sniffed, but he didn't smell smoke. Could it be a police car? Or an ambulance?

He took out his notepad and began to write.

Stan's Journal: Sunday, December 10. 8:45 p.m.

Red glow in cemetery. Beyond Deadman's Hill. No unusual sounds or smells. I'm on my way to check it out.

Deadman's Hill was one of Stan's favorite spots. In the winter, it was great for sledding—steep and smooth. On summer nights, he liked to lie on the hill and look at the stars.

It didn't scare him that the hill was in a

graveyard. He'd always lived right next to Hilltop Cemetery. It seemed like part of his yard. The cemetery was filled with tall trees and was very peaceful.

He'd heard lots of scary stories about the place. It was haunted by ghosts for example. But none had ever bothered him.

Stan reached the start of the hill. He flashed his light again. This side of the hill was clear, so he started to climb. The oldest graves in the cemetery were at the top of the slope.

Halfway up he stopped and looked around. The red glow looked strange as he got closer. It wasn't like a regular light. It was moving slowly. Up and down. Almost as if it were dancing.

Stan's Journal: Sunday, December 10. 8:48 p.m.

Getting closer to the glow. Haven't reached the top of the hill yet. Clear night. Cool but no wind.

Stan kept climbing. But as he got near the top, he slowed down. Something wasn't right. He could feel it. The glow had changed. It wasn't nearly as bright now.

He walked as softly as he could. Soon he reached the top of the hill. He stayed behind some trees and tried to see down the other side of the slope.

The glow was coming from a ball of light. It was about the size of a van, and it looked like a patch of fog. Except that it was red and glowing—and moving!

The fog swirled. It lifted and seemed to float. It got a little brighter as it moved along the slope. It was at least fifty yards away.

Stan took a step forward to see better. He stepped on a fallen branch, and it broke with a snap.

At the sound of the snap, the fog lost most of its glow. Stan could barely see it now. It was much smaller and dimmer. It had shrunk to about the size of a basketball.

Stan held his breath. Had the glow heard him? Was it trying to hide?

He watched for several minutes. The fog grew bright again. It began to expand and move. Soon it was bouncing near the bottom of the slope. Almost like it was dancing again.

Slowly and quietly, Stan took out his notepad.

Stan's Journal: Sunday, December 10. 8:55 p.m.

No fire. No electric lights. No source for the glow that I can see. Strange fog? It almost seems alive. Will try to get a closer look.

Stan took one very slow step forward. The glow stayed the same. So he took another step. And another. His foot crushed a pine cone with a crack. The red fog stopped moving.

Stan felt a chill. Was the fog aware that he was watching?

What is that thing? he wondered. He waited a moment. Then he took another step. The glow became much dimmer and smaller.

Stan reached into his pocket and grabbed his flashlight. He clicked it on but kept the light beam against his chest. He watched for a change in the red glow. Nothing happened for several minutes.

Stan lifted the flashlight and pointed the beam at the glow. Instantly, the glow became bigger and much brighter. It sped up the slope toward Stan.

Stan turned to run. Something was holding him back. The fog had reached out with what looked like a bright red hand. The hand grabbed Stan.

"Let go!" Stan yelled. He twisted and jumped. He managed to get free.

Stan ran down the hill toward home. He glanced back only once. The glow looked like flames now. It was bright red and angry. But it had stayed near the top of the hill.

Stan kept sprinting until he reached his house. He ducked into the garage and turned on the light.

His jacket seemed okay. There were sooty smudges where that thing had grabbed him. But there were no rips or other damage.

Stan caught his breath and walked into the house. He went straight up the stairs to his room. He could see Deadman's Hill from his window, but there was no sign of that glow.

He'd never seen anything like that, and he'd been watching the cemetery for years.

Some kind of ghoul, for sure, he thought. *That thing had awareness.*

Stan's Journal: Sunday, December 10. 9:17 p.m.

It had me in its grip. I got away, but it was mean. All I did was shine my light on it. Why did that disturb it so much? I'll have to talk this one over with the Zombie Hunters tomorrow.

I've never heard of a living thing that would glow like that. Or move so fast. I think I met up with something scarier than a ghost. I just came into contact with one of the undead!

Chapter 2:
The New Girl

Stan got to school early the next morning. He looked around the grounds. He wanted to talk to his best friend, Jared Jensen. He'd also round up Mitch Morris and Barry Bannon. The four boys each lived on the edge of a cemetery. They liked to share scary things they'd seen and heard.

They'd named their group the Zombie Hunters. Stan didn't have much else in common with Mitch or Barry. But talking about ghosts was fun, and they knew a lot about them.

There were four cemeteries in the town of Marshfield, which was sometimes called "Graveyard City." Stan lived by Hilltop Cemetery. Jared lived on the edge of Woodland Cemetery. Mitch's house was next to Evergreen Cemetery. Barry lived on the edge of Marshfield Grove.

Stan sat on a bench and waited for the others to show up. He saw a girl standing nearby and waved slightly. She smiled and walked over.

The girl was new to Marshfield. She'd moved in just two weeks earlier. She lived about a block away from Stan's house on Washington Street. Her yard backed up to Hilltop Cemetery, too.

"Hi, Stan," she said. She took a seat on the same bench.

"Hi," Stan said. He was a little embarrassed that she knew his name. He didn't know hers. They weren't in any of the same classes.

"I'm Amy Martinez," she said. "I live right near you."

"Right," Stan said. "How do you like the neighborhood?"

"It's great," she said. "Living with a cemetery behind the house is fantastic. There's so much spooky energy!"

Stan nodded. He'd felt that energy in a very real way last night. But he wouldn't tell Amy about that. He didn't want to let her know that he'd been scared.

"We were living in the city until last month," Amy said. "There were so many street lights and buildings that it never really got dark. The nights are so dark here. I love it. Some nights I just stare out the window at the graveyard."

"Me too," Stan said. "Sometimes I even go out there in the dark."

"Cool," Amy said. "I'd love to do that. Do you ever see ghosts?"

Stan shifted a bit. He looked around, but none of the guys were in sight. "Sometimes," he said softly. "It's no big deal. The place is haunted. That's for sure."

"Let me know if you ever want company," Amy said, grabbing Stan's arm. Then she let go. "I mean, if that would be okay."

Stan stood up in a hurry. He saw Jared walking toward the school. "Jared!" he shouted. "Wait up." Stan began to walk away.

"Nice talking to you," Amy called.

Stan turned quickly. "Yeah," he said. "I have to go."

He caught up to Jared and filled him in about the reddish fog. By the time he finished, the late bell was ringing. So they hurried into their sixth grade classroom.

During the first class, the students were supposed to do research for a paper about local history. Stan had already done a lot of research. He took out his notepad instead to write down a few thoughts.

Stan's Journal: Monday, December 11. 8:51 a.m.

Jared said we should find some way to protect ourselves from the red fog. Then we can watch it and figure out what it is. He said if it's dangerous, we need to get rid of it like we did with those grave robber ghosts he had over in Woodland Cemetery. I have no idea how we would do that with the fog since it doesn't seem to have a full body.

I met the new neighbor, Amy. What does she mean by "spooky energy?" How much does she know about Hilltop Cemetery?

At lunchtime, Stan found Mitch and Barry. He described the fog to them. "It grabbed me," he said.

"How could fog grab you?" Mitch asked with a sneer.

"This wasn't regular fog," Stan said. "It was as if it were alive. Like it saw me and heard me. And it definitely chased me!"

18

"I've seen all kinds of things in those cemeteries," Barry said. "Werewolves, zombies, plain old ghosts. But never anything like that!"

Mitch laughed. "Maybe it was smoke from somebody's grill," he said. "They were cooking hot dogs or salmon. Something pink."

Stan shook his head. "Laugh it off if you want," he said. "I know what I saw. And it was creepy."

Mitch put a fist on the table. "Don't worry," he said. "We always come through. We'll help you figure this out."

"Nothing spooks us," Barry said. "We'll scare whatever it is right back where it came from."

But Stan knew better. He'd seen Mitch and Barry scared plenty of times. They acted tough, but ghosts had a way of making anybody shiver.

I need help from somebody who won't

freak out, Stan thought. He'd ask Jared to check things out with him tonight. Mitch and Barry might be helpful later. For now, Stan wanted to do this quietly.

I don't want to stir up trouble, he thought. Whatever that fog was, it didn't want to be disturbed. It had only reacted badly when he shined the light on it. It had almost seemed shy before that—like it wanted to be left alone.

Chapter 3:
Woodland Cemetery

Stan walked home from school with Jared. It was out of his way, but he wanted to talk more about the red fog.

"Sometimes fog gets trapped in a valley," Jared said. "It can just sit there if the weather conditions are right. Maybe the moon was shining on it. That's what made it glow."

"The moon wasn't up yet," Stan said. "And the fog didn't sit there. It was floating up and down. As if it were dancing or exploring. And I told you, it came after me. It grabbed me!"

Jared nodded. "I'd like to see that for myself. But I can't tonight. I have karate practice. I won't be home until late."

"That's okay," Stan said. "Maybe we'll do it tomorrow night."

They'd reached Jared's house. Stan could get home the fastest by cutting through Woodland Cemetery. He took a path at the far end that led to Hilltop Cemetery.

Stan decided to make a few more notes. He'd get a better look at the other side of Deadman's Hill in daylight. The sun wouldn't be down for another half hour.

He walked briskly toward the hill. The wind had picked up. Dry leaves swirled around him. The grass was all brown.

Woodland was an old cemetery. Most of the gravestones were gray granite. A few had toppled over. Many were covered with moss.

When Stan reached the path that led to Hilltop, he began to run. He wanted to be out of the cemetery before dark.

Soon he'd reached the patch of woods at the top of Deadman's Hill. He stopped to write some notes.

Stan's Journal: Monday, December 11. 4:19 p.m.

No signs of any fire. Nothing unusual. The bushes down the hill look healthy. I don't think the red glow hurt them. Up here where the big, red hand grabbed me seems the same, too.

I know this cemetery is haunted. That's never bothered me before. Especially during the day.

They only come out at night, right? That's what they say about ghosts…

Stan heard something moving down below. He shoved his notepad in his pocket. He didn't see anything, but the bushes were moving. He reached for a big stick and held it tightly. He also held his breath.

The bushes moved again, and someone stepped out onto the grass. Stan let out his breath. It was Amy!

"Hey!" he called. "What are you doing?"

"Hi, Stan," Amy said. She waved and started walking up the hill.

"What were you doing down there?" Stan asked.

Amy shrugged. "I just decided to take a walk," she said. "Talking about the cemetery with you sparked my interest."

Stan pointed toward the bushes at the bottom of the hill. "But why were you in there?" he asked.

Amy looked down the hill. She seemed to be thinking hard. "I don't know," she said. "I just felt drawn to that spot."

Stan felt a shiver. Why would she be drawn to that very place? Just one day after he had seen the fog there?

"Remember how I said I felt spooky energy coming from this cemetery?" Amy said.

Stan nodded.

"When I got home from school, I felt it again. It was a really strong feeling," Amy said. "Almost as if it were calling me to come out here. Have you ever felt that way?"

"Not exactly," Stan said. "In fact, I felt the opposite last night. Right here. As if something wanted me to go away."

Amy hugged herself. "That's strange," she said. "And kind of scary. What did you do?"

"I left as fast as I could." He didn't mention being grabbed.

Amy looked back down the hill. "There's something odd down there," she said. "I didn't see anything or hear anything. But it felt like I was being watched. As if a panther or a wolf was hiding nearby."

"But you said you heard something calling you," Stan said.

"Not out loud." Amy put her hand to her chin. She didn't say anything more for a moment. "I just felt this strong sense that I should go out there," she finally said.

"I'd be careful if I were you," Stan said. He didn't want to tell Amy about the red fog. But what if she came out here by herself again? At night? He knew he had to warn her.

"Last night I saw this strange red glow," he said. "Right in that very spot you were exploring. It seemed harmless enough. But when I shined a light on it, it attacked me. I was lucky to get away."

"The glow attacked you?" Amy asked. "How could that be?"

Stan shrugged. "It reached out a hand and grabbed me. I got away, but just barely."

"Wow," Amy said. "I'd like to see that."

"I'd stay clear of this place at night," Stan said. "I don't know what that thing was. But it was angry, I can tell you that."

"How could a fog hurt you?" she asked. "Or a glow?"

"This thing had strength," Stan said. "I have no idea what it was. But I wouldn't want to mess with it again."

It was nearly dark now. Stan was eager to get home. "Let's get out of here," he said. "I'll tell you more about it sometime. But promise me that you won't come out here alone. Not at night anyway."

"Okay," Amy said.

Stan wasn't convinced that she'd stay away. He tried to get her to think about something else.

"Why did your family leave the city?" he asked as they walked.

"My mom always wanted to move back to Marshfield," Amy said. "She grew up here. Her family had lived here since way back. So when a job opened up at the hospital, she took it."

%%%%%%%%%%%%%%%%%%%%%%

After dinner, Stan remembered that he'd meant to make more notes. Meeting Amy in the graveyard had kept him from doing that. So he went up to his room.

Stan's Journal: Monday, December 11. 7:22 p.m.

Amy said she'd been lured to the very spot where I saw the fog. Not sure what she means. She didn't seem scared at all. She should be.

The top of Deadman's Hill has the oldest graves in Hilltop Cemetery. Most of them are at least 200 years old. As you move down the slope, the graves aren't as old. The newer graves are on the other side of the cemetery.

I love looking at the old gravestones. I wonder what those people's lives were like. So long ago. What are their spirits doing now? I know that some of them aren't resting!

Stan heard the doorbell ring. A minute later, there was a knock on his door.

"Stan," his mother said, "there's someone downstairs to see you."

He opened the door. "Who?" he asked. But he already knew.

His mom smiled. "The new girl on the street. Amy? She asked if you could help her with something."

Stan frowned. He knew what she wanted. "I'm kind of busy," he said.

His mom put her hand on Stan's shoulder. "I'm sure it won't take long," she said. "Go on. Be a good neighbor."

"Okay," Stan reluctantly replied.

He looked around his room. He wanted to bring something to protect him from that fog.

But how do you protect yourself from the undead? He had no idea about that. So he let out a sigh and headed downstairs. He had a bad feeling in his gut.

Chapter 4:
Playtime

Amy laughed as they stepped onto the street. "Did you tell your mom I needed help with my homework?" she asked.

"No. But I guess she figured that."

"Yeah. I said I was working on a project," Amy said.

Stan winced. "I don't lie to my mom."

Amy smiled. "I didn't either."

Stan gave her a mean look.

"I didn't!" Amy said. "This *is* a project. I didn't say it was for school."

Returning to the graveyard didn't seem like a good idea to Stan. He knew that thing was aware of them.

"We have to be very quiet," he said. "Completely silent."

"I figured that," Amy said. "It's best to go through my yard. Whatever chased you last night might be waiting for you again. We'll try to sneak up on it."

They reached Amy's house. "No one's home," she said. "My mom is working. Dad's at a meeting."

They walked along the driveway and into the yard. Washington Street was curved. From Amy's yard, they could approach Deadman's Hill from a different angle.

"Are you ready?" Amy asked.

Stan nodded. "Let's go." He took a few soft steps.

Amy went much more quickly. She was soon several feet ahead.

"Slow down," Stan whispered. "It'll hear you."

Amy waited for him to catch up. "I'm quiet," she said. "My feet don't make much noise."

It was true. Even though they were walking on dry leaves, Amy's footsteps seemed to make no sound.

"How do you do that?" he asked. "Are you wearing slippers or something?"

Amy laughed. "I'm just light on my feet."

Stan followed her into the graveyard. The leaves crunched lightly under his shoes until they reached the grass.

Amy leaned toward him. "Let's go through the woods," she said. "We'll circle around the other side of the hill."

Stan shrugged. Amy seemed to know her way around the graveyard already.

The sky was cloudy. Things were even darker than the night before. Stan pulled up the hood of his sweatshirt and tied it tight.

They didn't speak for a while. Despite the dark, Amy made her way swiftly through the woods. Stan had to hurry to keep up. Twice he nearly tripped over fallen logs.

They were getting close to the bushes at the bottom of the hill. The ground was usually damp and soft here. But it hadn't rained for several weeks. Everything was dry.

Stan kneeled. He could see all the way up the hill. He didn't see anything glowing. No sign of the fog.

Amy held up her hand. She seemed to be saying, *Just wait.*

The ground felt cold under Stan's knees. There had been no snow yet this winter, but the nights were getting colder.

"Look there," Amy whispered, pointing to a spot about halfway up the hill.

Stan looked toward a very large gravestone. It seemed to be shining more than the ones around it. The glow was slightly pink.

Amy put her finger to her lips. "Shhhh," she said.

I know that, Stan thought. *Does she think I'm stupid enough to make noise at a time like this?*

As he watched, the glow formed into a ball. It floated out from behind the gravestone.

The glow was no bigger than a softball this time. It looked like the steam from a teakettle, except that it was pink.

The glow moved onto the grassy slope. It floated toward the ground slowly. Then it rose toward the lowest branches of the trees.

Stan bit down on his lip. He kept his eyes open wide, never looking away from the glow. It seemed to be searching for something.

Slowly the glow grew bigger and brighter. It began moving more quickly. It bounced on the slope and flipped over backward. It seemed to be enjoying the activity.

Amy spoke. Her voice was so low that Stan could barely hear it. He leaned closer to her.

"This is nuts," she said. "It's playing!"

"I think it's dancing," Stan said.

Amy giggled. "Whatever. It's having fun."

Suddenly the glow stopped moving. It seemed to focus on the spot where Amy and Stan were hiding. It shrank to the size of a basketball. But it became brighter, like a flame.

Amy moved back. She grabbed Stan's arm.

"It heard us," she whispered.

"Just stay still."

Stan got off his knees. He crouched on his heels, getting ready to jump up and run. He held his breath.

The glow became a little dimmer. Slowly, it began floating across the slope again. And it got bigger.

Stan gulped. He turned to face Amy. "Seen enough?" he whispered.

Amy nodded.

They stood and backed away. Stan kept his eyes on the glow. He walked carefully. But he bumped into a pine tree. The branches shook and made a soft rustling sound.

As if it had heard the sound, the glow stopped moving. It grew bigger. Then it split into several smaller balls of light. Some went up the hill. Two went to the sides. Another came down the hill toward them!

"Run!" Stan said. He turned on his flashlight and shined it toward the ground.

As soon as he started to run, his hand brushed another tree. The flashlight fell.

I'll get that tomorrow, Stan thought. There was no way he was spending another second in this graveyard tonight.

Stan and Amy reached an open field. Stan caught up to Amy and they sprinted. They were halfway to Amy's yard when a ball of blue light came flying toward their heads.

"Duck!" Stan yelled.

The light flew past. It vanished.

Another light came flying in from the left. This one was yellow. It swooped past them. Then it circled back and floated next to Stan as he ran.

"Jump!" yelled Amy.

A green light was coming toward their feet. Stan leaped as it arrived. The light dodged and missed him.

"This is crazy!" Stan said. He was puffing hard. But he kept running as fast as he could. He dodged away from flying lights all the way to Amy's yard.

"Come in," Amy said, running up her back steps.

They shut the kitchen door. Stan leaned against a chair and wiped the sweat from his face.

"They were trying to kill us," he said.

Amy let out her breath and shook her head. She sat in a chair across from Stan and said, "I don't think so."

"You don't? Those things were aiming right at us. They just missed us!"

Amy gave Stan a half smile. "I think they would have hit us if they wanted to. They dodged away at the last second every time."

Stan sat down. He placed both palms on the kitchen table. "So what are you saying?" he asked. "They were just trying to scare us?"

Amy shrugged. "I think they wanted

to play," she said. "It was like tag. Or dodgeball."

"Or a war zone," Stan said. "I think they were aiming at us. We just barely escaped."

Amy laughed. "We're not that quick," she said. "They would have nailed us if they wanted to. I say they were playing."

Stan touched his chin with his hand. He had to think about this. Whatever had grabbed him the night before was not playing. He didn't believe that these were either.

Still, Amy might be right. The lights were fast and seemed to be in control. They could have hit him every time.

So what was it they wanted?

And what in the world were they?

Chapter 5:
Flying V

Stan's Journal: Monday, December 11 . 10:37 p.m.

Can't sleep. Keep looking out at the cemetery. All is quiet and dark.

Strangest night of my life. Bombarded by flying lights. The red glow split into many. All different colors.

Every light seemed to be "alive" in some way.

The big question: Were they playing? Were they attacking? Were they angry or joyful? Very hard to tell.

I'm not even sure I want to know.

Stan spent a long time looking out the window. A few times he thought he saw a glow in the cemetery. But he wasn't sure.

He kept coming back to one thought. The fog that had grabbed him the night before was angry. It had wanted to harm him. But tonight it had seemed different.

Because Amy was there, he decided. She'd been the difference. That force could have hurt them if it wanted to. It had split into many different lights. Any of them could have flown into him if they had wanted. But they didn't.

The more he thought about it, the more he thought she'd been right. They were playing.

But what would they do next time? What if they found Stan alone? Would they want to play then? Or would they try to finish him off?

Stan's Journal: Monday, December 11. 11:38 p.m.

How did that glow split into so many balls of light? Were the lights controlled by one mind? Or did they all have minds of their own?

The light I saw on Sunday night seemed like one force. It stayed whole. But could it have been many forces? Why did they stay together? Maybe that keeps them safe. Maybe they stay together like a family. Or a community. And they split up when they need to. For fun. Or a battle.

Stan shivered, but he wasn't cold. He knew that he needed to sleep soon. There was school tomorrow.

He turned off his bedroom light. Then he stepped to the window for one last look.

The moon had risen. There were still a lot of clouds. But there was more light in the cemetery.

He could see the top of Deadman's Hill. A faint red ball was floating there.

Stan gulped. It was back.

He watched for several minutes. The light grew brighter. It floated down this side of the hill, closer to Stan's house. *Was it exploring again?*

It moved slowly. As if it were looking for something. It came nearly all the way to Stan's yard.

Where is my flashlight? Stan thought. Then he remembered. It was out in the cemetery. Probably still lit and draining the batteries.

He wished he had a light. That glowing force seemed to hate having a light shined on it. That's why it had attacked him the night before.

He quietly made his way out of his bedroom. His parents were asleep. He went slowly down the stairs and opened a kitchen drawer. There was a small flashlight. He took it to his room.

Maybe this will scare that glow away for now, he thought. He opened his window.

He could see the red glow. It was only a few feet away from the backyard.

He turned on the light and aimed it. The beam was weak. He could hardly see where it touched the trees at the edge of the cemetery.

He turned off the beam. He shook the flashlight. But when he turned it on again, the beam was even weaker.

Stan looked at the yard again. The glow had split into five orange balls of light. They were lined up in a V shape. Like an arrow. The point of the arrow was aiming straight at him!

Stan slammed down the window. He shut the blinds and turned on his bedroom light before jumping into bed.

He pulled the covers over his head. He was shaking. He'd sleep with his light on tonight.

If he ever got to sleep, that is.

Chapter 6:
Shedding Light on the Subject

"They were pointing straight at me," Stan said to Jared before school the next morning. Stan had told Jared everything that happened. "What do you think?" he asked. "Did they want me to come back out to play? Or were they aiming at me like a target?"

Jared shrugged. "No way to know for sure," he said. "It sounds like they acted different when Amy was there."

"I think so."

"It actually sounds pretty cool," Jared said. "At least the part when they were flying at you."

"Yeah," Stan said. "I guess that was exciting."

"I'll go out there with you after school," Jared said. "We'll see what happens when it gets dark. Should we bring Barry and Mitch?"

Stan thought it over. It might be safer with all four Zombie Hunters. But Mitch and Barry would try to act tough. They'd make that thing angry.

"Let's leave them out of this for now," Stan said.

He tried to avoid Amy all day. She finally came up to him as he was leaving for home.

"Fun time last night, wasn't it?" she said.

"Some of it," Stan said. "That thing came back later. It was close to my window. It was split into five orange balls this time."

Amy smiled. "Wow! They just floated around?"

"No. It was like they were staring at me."

"Oh." Amy pointed in the direction of Washington Street. "Are you walking home?" she asked.

Stan looked around. He didn't see Jared. "I guess," he said. "I can drop off my backpack. But then I have to go out. I'd stay away from the graveyard if I were you."

Amy shrugged. "You keep saying that, but I'm not scared."

"I know. But I still wouldn't go out there alone."

"So, you'll go with me?" Amy asked.

"I just told you. I have to do something."

"Later then? After dinner?" Amy prodded.

Stan knew that he had to agree. He'd

visit the graveyard with her tonight. That way, she wouldn't go out there this afternoon. He could check things out with Jared first without her around.

"Okay," he said. "If you promise to stay home this afternoon, we can go out there tonight."

"I promise." Amy rolled her eyes.

She thinks I'm a wimp, Stan thought. *I don't care. I just don't want her bothering me now.*

"So you'll wait until later?" Stan said. "I'll meet you after dinner. By your house. About seven thirty?"

"Okay," Amy said. "I have some homework to do this afternoon anyway. And it's much more fun being out there at night."

Stan had made plans to meet Jared at four o'clock. He'd walk through Hilltop Cemetery. Jared would walk through Woodland Cemetery. They'd meet on the path between the two graveyards.

Stan's Journal: Tuesday, December 12. 3:50 p.m.

It was hard to get rid of Amy. She thinks the lights are harmless. I don't. Those are dead spirits. Maybe they want to take over my body since they have none of their own. Yes, they can be playful. But I also think they're dangerous. Maybe I can figure out a way to get rid of them.

Before they get rid of me.

He had to hurry. Jared would be waiting. And the sun was already going down. It would be dark in less than an hour.

He put his notepad in his pocket. Then he hurried downstairs and out the back door. He looked around. He didn't want Amy to see him going toward the cemetery.

He ran across the grass, dodging past gravestones. He ran by Deadman's Hill. Then, he cut up toward the woods.

Soon he could see Jared ahead on the path. He waved for him to come over.

"Did you find the flashlight?" Jared asked.

"I didn't look yet," Stan said. "I didn't want Amy following me."

"Why would she?"

"Because she doesn't want to miss anything," Stan said. "She thinks the lights are friendly."

"Maybe they are."

"And maybe not." Stan started walking quickly back toward Deadman's Hill.

"So, did this thing make any sounds?" Jared asked.

Stan had to think about that. It was silent while it was floating around. But did the smaller lights make noise as they attacked?

"I don't think so," Stan said. "I was running so fast I might not have noticed. Why?"

"A sound might tell us something," Jared said. "If it was laughing, it might have been playing. If it was whistling like a bullet, that might be anger."

Stan led the way down Deadman's Hill to the bushes. He pointed. "I dropped the flashlight in there," he said.

"Let's get it."

Stan headed for the pine trees. He pulled back some branches. But he didn't see the flashlight.

"It has to be around here," he said. "I bumped into this tree and dropped it."

"Are you sure this is the right tree?" Jared asked.

"Pretty sure." Stan looked around. "It was dark out. But, we were right near here."

"Let's spread out," Jared said. "We'll find it."

This is the spot, Stan thought. He kneeled in the dirt. Halfway up the hill was that large gravestone. This was where he'd been last night.

"I found it!" Jared called.

Stan turned to look. Jared was about forty feet away, in a dense patch of trees. *But we weren't over there,* Stan thought. *Not at all.*

He walked toward Jared.

"The batteries are dead," Jared said, turning the button on and off several times.

"It was on all night," Stan said. "All day, too."

"Do you have any new ones?" Jared asked.

Stan shrugged. "I don't think so. Do you?"

"Probably," Jared said. "My dad always has stuff like that. You can borrow some."

"Great." Stan looked up at the trees. Then he scanned the ground. There were lots of rocks and holes. There was no way he'd been in this spot last night. He would have fallen in the dark. "You think it could have rolled over here from those bushes?"

"No way," Jared said. "The ground's

too rough."

Stan shook his head. "Very strange," he said. "Let's go get those batteries. I need that light."

As they turned to go, Jared tripped over one of the rocks. He put out his hands and braced himself. But his foot was stuck.

"Yow!" he said as he went down. His foot came loose, and he grabbed it.

"Are you okay?" Stan asked.

Jared winced. "I think so," he said. "Help me up. I twisted my ankle."

With Jared limping, it took a long time to get to his house.

"Let's have the batteries," Stan said. He looked at the sky. It was nearly dark. "I need to get home. I don't like crossing the cemetery at night."

"You'll be fine," Jared said. "You'll have the flashlight."

Right, Stan thought. *They hate the light.* He couldn't quite figure that out. They were made of light. Why would they hate having light shined on them?

"I guess you'll be staying in tonight," Stan said.

"Yeah. I'd better ice this foot or it'll swell."

Stan had expected Jared to join him in the graveyard. Now it would be just him and Amy.

That was probably better. The force seemed to like her.

There was just one other thing bothering him. Who had moved that flashlight? And why?

Chapter 7:
Game Over

Almost dark. I have to cut through two graveyards. Wish Jared was with me. Cold breeze blowing. Lots of clouds. Feels like it could snow.

Stan rubbed his hands together. His gloves were thin. The cold bit right through them.

He turned on the flashlight and started to jog. The path went up a hill, then down. Then there was another big hill before Hilltop Cemetery began.

56

Stan's feet made a *pat, pat* sound on the dirt path as he ran. The wind shook the branches of the trees.

As he reached the top of the hill, he looked up. *Oh no,* he thought.

Just as he had feared, the red glow was back. It was floating above the path. Stan stopped short. He turned off the flashlight so the red light wouldn't get angry. He looked to his left. He could cut down a steep slope to get away.

And then the glow reached out a hand. It didn't grab for Stan this time. It made a motion to wave him over. Just like Stan had done earlier when he met Jared.

"No way!" Stan said. He stepped off the path and headed down the steeper hill. But now a blue glow was blocking his way.

Stan looked back. Could he run to Jared's house? He took a quick step in that direction. A yellow glow appeared in his path.

Stan was surrounded. The safest path was the one he'd started on. He raced uphill to it. A smaller red glow was still there. Stan ran straight toward it.

"Out of my way!" he yelled.

The red ball floated up and Stan ran beneath it. A purple light came flying at him from his right.

Stan dodged. The light flew past. But a blue one came in from his left.

He kept running. Balls of light zoomed toward his head, but they always missed. Stan was soon sweating and panting.

They keep missing, he thought. And then he knew that Amy had been right. They were playing!

Stan laughed. He threw himself at a green ball of light. He missed, and he rolled to the ground. He swatted his hand at another purple ball. Then he hopped up and started running again.

All the way home, the misty lights stayed with him. They flew past his head. They came at his legs so he had to jump over them.

It was like a game of football. Or tag.

What a blast, he thought.

Finally Stan stopped running. He was out of breath. And he was nearly home.

"What are you?" Stan said to a yellow ball that was floating a few feet away. "Can you hear me?"

The light didn't move. It began to fade. Within a few seconds, Stan couldn't see it at all.

He glanced around. A purple light was fading over to his left. And the larger red light was halfway up Deadman's Hill. It was getting dimmer by the second.

"Game's over, I guess," Stan said. "Catch your breath. We'll be back out in a couple hours."

He took several steps toward his house. The evening was already quite dark. He hit the button of the flashlight, but it wouldn't go on.

Is it jammed? Stan wondered. But the button seemed to work fine. Those new batteries must be bad.

"Thanks for nothing, Jared," Stan said.

He looked back. The glowing lights were gone. They'd given him a good scare at first. But maybe they were nothing to worry about after all.

Chapter 8:
Yellow vs. Orange

Snow flurries. Not enough to cover the ground yet. Meeting Amy in ten minutes. This could be fun tonight. It's like laser tag. Too bad Jared got hurt. He would have liked it. Those things are fast. Still haven't heard them make a sound. They seem very smart. And playful.

"You were right," Stan said as he walked up to Amy. "They chased me all the way across the cemetery today. But it was cool."

"Wait a minute!" Amy said. "You made me promise not to go out there alone. But you did?"

Stan blushed. "I had to," he said. "I was at Jared's house. I was late for dinner. I had to cut through or my mom would have been mad. She'd have made me stay in tonight."

"Sure," Amy said. "Did you find your flashlight?"

"Yeah, but it isn't working."

"I have one," she said. "Let's go."

They came around the far side of Deadman's Hill again. "Think they'll be waiting for us?" Amy asked.

"Probably. They love to play."

It was snowing harder now. The wind had died down. Amy shined her light on the ground as they entered the woods. She started to jog.

As they came into a clearing, Stan looked at the hill. The big red glow was halfway up the slope. Amy turned off her flashlight.

"There's just one of them," Stan whispered.

"It will probably split when we start playing," Amy said. "Should we chase it?"

Stan felt a shiver. He wasn't so sure now. The light seemed to be staring at them. Something about it didn't seem right.

"Maybe we'll approach it slowly," he said. "We'll see how it reacts."

He started walking up the hill. The light grew a bit smaller. It floated farther up the slope.

"It's just shy," Amy said.

"Or else it's getting ready to attack."

"Come on!" Amy said. She started running toward the glow.

Stan stayed back. As Amy got closer to the glow, it became much smaller. Soon it was the size of a baseball. It was very bright. It had lifted up to the top of a pine tree. Amy stopped running and stared at it.

Stan walked up. He brushed a few snowflakes from his face. "It's not playing," he said softly.

"It will," Amy said. She tilted her head back to see it better. "What are you doing, Red?"

The red glow got bigger. But it stayed up high.

"It doesn't seem very friendly now," Stan whispered.

"It's just checking us out," Amy answered. "It's shy, remember? It wants to make sure we won't hurt it."

"How could we hurt it?" Stan said. "It's fast and powerful."

Amy clicked on her flashlight. She aimed it at the ground, but she smiled. "Hi, Red," she said. She clicked the light on and off several times.

The red glow moved behind a branch, as if it were hiding.

"It hates the light," Stan said.

"I see you, Red!" Amy called. "You can't get away from me."

She shined her light at the tree trunk. She slowly raised it, and the beam moved up toward the red glow.

"I wouldn't do that!" Stan said. The glow was turning brighter. It was pulsing. The flashlight beam had almost reached it.

The glow burst into hundreds of tiny balls of light. They quickly spread out over the graveyard.

"Wow," Amy said. "How cool."

Stan didn't think it was cool. The lights were swarming now, like slow-moving bees. They were high overhead, but getting closer.

The lights were many colors. Red and blue and orange. Some were green or yellow. They swirled around the snowflakes, casting light on them, too.

"So pretty," Amy said. "Like tiny fireworks."

Stan took a few steps back. "I think we should get out of here," he said.

"Why?" Amy replied. "It's playtime!"

The tiny lights had gathered near the top of the hill. They bobbed up and down, mixing their colors. There was a thin layer of snow on the ground now. It reflected some of the lights.

Stan gulped. "Amy," he said, "we should leave while we have the chance."

She laughed. "Let's charge them."

"Are you crazy?"

"No. I think that's what they're waiting for. They want us to start the game."

Stan took another step back. But Amy raced up the hill.

The lights drew into a tight pack. Then they came shooting down. They flew over Amy's head and swooped low as they got near Stan.

Stan turned and ran. The lights overtook him. He was surrounded. A red one zipped close to his ear. Blue and green ones came close to his body. A purple one aimed for his legs.

Stan hit a snowy spot and slipped. As he fell to the ground, an orange light smacked into his face. It burned.

Stan rolled on the grass and grabbed for his cheek. He rubbed it hard. The spot where the light had hit stung.

Stan sat up. Another orange one was flying toward him. He covered his head with both hands and went down.

The orange light bounced off his neck. That spot burned, too. Stan fell face-first onto the grass. Orange lights pelted his coat and his legs.

"Get off!" Stan yelled, kicking at the lights. "Leave me alone."

They weren't playing this time. It seemed as if they wanted to hurt him. But why?

Stan got to his knees. He swung his

arms and the orange lights backed off. A group of lights floated above him. They came together as a big red glow again.

Amy ran down the hill and knelt next to Stan. "Did they hurt you?" she asked.

Stan rubbed his neck. "Some," he said. "Like a burn. Did they get you, too?"

"No," she said. "They all went straight at you."

Stan raised a fist and shook it at the red glow. "What's your problem?" he asked. "I didn't do anything to you."

The glow floated up the hill and stayed near the top. Stan stared at it for a minute. "Ready to leave now?" he said to Amy.

"Think they'll let us go?"

Stan stood up. "There's only one way to find out," he said. "Come on."

The glow stayed where it was. Stan and Amy began walking home. Stan looked back every few seconds to make sure they weren't being followed.

"They swarmed all over you," Amy said. "You're lucky those yellow lights were there."

"What do you mean?"

"The yellow ones were trying to protect you. They were blocking the orange ones."

"They were?"

"Yeah. Couldn't you tell?"

Stan shook his head. "I was just trying to protect myself. The orange ones hurt when they hit me."

He stopped walking. They'd reached the edge of the woods. Stan gazed back at the hill. The red glow was still there, but it was small and dim.

"What were the other ones doing?" he asked.

"What other ones?" Amy said.

"You said the orange ones were attacking me. The yellow ones were blocking them. What were the other colors doing?"

"They were being playful," Amy said.

"It was very strange to watch. But the yellow and orange ones were fighting each other. The others looked like they were having fun."

The snow had stopped. Stan felt his cheek. A small spot was sore, like sunburn. His neck stung a little, too. But he wasn't really hurt.

"You're the one who got them mad," Stan said. "By shining that light at them. Why didn't they attack you?"

"Who knows?" Amy smiled. "I guess they like me better."

Why wouldn't they like me? Stan wondered. He looked back again. The red glow was floating near that big gravestone on the hill. A few tiny orange lights were moving about. They looked like bees around a hive.

Stan stared at the scene for a minute.

Amy grabbed his arm and pulled. "What are you waiting for?" she asked.

Stan shook out of her grip. "Nothing," he said. "Just thinking. The funny thing is, I didn't see any orange ones this afternoon. The ones I was playing with were many different colors. But none of them were orange."

He was starting to get an idea. He needed to get a closer look at that big gravestone in the middle of the hill. The glow always seemed to start there.

As soon as the sun comes up, I'll take a look, he thought. *Maybe that stone will tell me something.*

He started walking faster. "Let's get away from those things while we can," he said. "They still look angry to me."

Chapter 9:
The Chapmans

Stan's Journal: Wednesday, December 13. 6:17 a.m.

The sun isn't up yet, but the sky is getting lighter. Just a dusting of snow out there. Cold morning.

Didn't sleep well. Every time I dozed off, I saw those swarming lights.

The burns on my cheek and neck aren't bad. Just little orange spots. Not very sore.

Stan went down to the kitchen. His father was getting ready to leave for work.

"Hey," Stan said.

"Morning," said his dad. "You're up early. You hungry?"

"Not really." Stan reached for a banana and started to peel it. "I just wanted to see the snow."

"You'll see plenty," his dad said. "We're supposed to get a couple of inches tonight."

"Oh well. It's winter."

Stan's dad set his coffee cup on the counter. "What did you do to your face?" he asked.

"Where?"

"That spot. Looks like a burn."

Stan put his hand to his cheek. "I don't know," he said. "It isn't much. I might have gotten splashed with some hot chocolate. Or soup."

His dad pushed Stan's hand away and looked at the spot. "Seems all right," he said. "Kind of an odd color though. Sort of orange."

Stan shrugged. "It'll heal."

"Sure it will." Stan's dad looked around the kitchen, then frowned. "Have you seen my glasses?"

Stan shook his head.

"They must be upstairs," his dad said.

Stan looked out the back door. As soon as his dad left, he'd go out to the graveyard. He needed to find out a few things before school.

Stan ran upstairs and got his notepad. He picked up the flashlight and clicked it on. This time it worked.

Must be a loose switch or something, he thought.

There was no wind, so the morning didn't seem cold at all. Stan walked quickly through his yard toward Deadman's Hill. He yawned.

The big gravestone was circled by many smaller ones. Carved in the big stone was the name Chapman. Below that were several names and dates. Stan copied them into his notepad.

FATHER

Jacob Chapman: 1875-1935

MOTHER

Abigail Chapman: 1879-1946

William: 1905-1918

Eldred: 1907-1918

Paul: 1909-1982

Winnie: 1911-1918

Wow, Stan thought. *Three kids from this family died in 1918. I wonder what happened.*

There were smaller gravestones lined up behind the big one. Each had the name of one of the Chapmans.

Stan walked to another group of gravestones. He found the sites for two more children who had died in 1918. Ellen Reed, age eleven. Henry Morris, age ten. Nearby he found several more.

What went wrong in 1918? he wondered. *This is very sad.*

Stan took a deep breath and let it out. The cemetery seemed so peaceful in the early morning. The light of the sun was casting long shadows from the trees.

Stan's Journal: Wednesday, December 13. 6:48 a.m.

Quiet day. No movement. No glowing lights. But I can feel the energy that Amy talked about. It's like I'm being watched. Or listened to. They seem to be all around me. None of them are visible. But they're here.

He walked down the back of the slope. When he reached the spot where he'd been attacked by the orange lights, he stopped. A few birds were chirping in the forest. Stan could smell the smoke from someone's fireplace not too far away.

He loved living by this cemetery. He knew he needed to solve this problem though. Things just weren't normal lately. Not at night anyway.

Stan noticed a man standing near the middle of the hill. He was an older man, dressed in a dark blue suit and a black necktie. Stan waved, but the man just stared at him. He looked angry.

Stan headed quickly toward home.

At school that morning, Stan asked for a pass to the computer lab. "To work on my local history project," he said. That was sort of true.

He sat at a terminal and typed "1918 deaths Marshfield."

The search engine returned a long list of Web sites. There were a few obituaries. One site was called "Marshfield Vital

Records 1918." And there was one called "1918 flu epidemic."

Stan clicked on that last one. He learned that many people around the world had become sick with the flu in 1918. It spread quickly. Millions of people died, including many children. The medicine wasn't very good at fighting the sickness.

Stan let out a low whistle. This was what he'd been looking for. Had the Chapmans and those other kids died of the flu? It seemed likely.

At lunch, he sat with the other Zombie Hunters. He told them about being attacked by the orange lights. But he didn't say anything about the flu.

"And the yellow lights protected you?" Mitch asked.

"It seemed that way," Stan said. "At least they tried to."

"But they all mash together sometimes?" Barry asked. "Into one big red glow?"

Stan nodded. "That's how it usually is. They only split up when they want to chase me. Or play."

"We should go out there tonight," Mitch said. "Bring tennis rackets or something to protect ourselves."

"That won't help," Stan said. "They can go right through anything."

"No problem," Mitch said. "I'm not afraid of ghostly lights."

"Neither am I," said Barry. "What can they do to us? Nothing."

Stan pointed at Barry. "Don't be so sure," he said. "They burned my neck and my face. It could have been a lot worse."

Barry made a fist. "I'll wear a hood tied real tight." He laughed. "Then all I'll have to protect is my nose."

Stan looked across at Jared. He hadn't said much. He gave Stan a serious look.

"How's the ankle?" Stan asked.

"Pretty sore," Jared answered. "I don't

think I could run if I had to. I'd better stay home tonight."

Stan nodded. Without Jared, he felt uneasy. Mitch and Barry knew a lot about ghosts, but they took way too many chances.

"Okay," Stan said. "Let's meet at eight thirty by the entrance to the cemetery."

He wasn't sure if he should tell Amy. She was a big part of this so far. But maybe it would go better without her tonight. He'd make up something to tell her.

I'll suggest we leave them alone for one night, he thought.

He knew that he should follow that advice, too. But it was too late. Mitch and Barry would never back out now.

Chapter 10:
Safety in Numbers

Stan's Journal: Wednesday, December 13. 8:18 p.m.

Checked my flashlight. It seems to be working now. I have a ski mask, so there won't be much exposed skin. Will that be enough to protect me from the orange lights?

Are these the ghosts of all those kids who died in 1918? Why can't they rest in peace? And why do some of them want to hurt me?

They don't speak, so I might never know the answers. But I do know that I won't be safe until I find some way to stop them. Or get rid of them. Or maybe just get them to like me.

The snow had started falling again as Stan left the house. He didn't go through the cemetery. Instead he walked along Washington Street to the main entrance. Mitch and Barry were waiting there.

"We weren't sure if you'd show," Mitch said with a laugh. "Thought you might be too scared."

"Nope," Stan said. "But you might be when you see these things."

"I doubt it," Mitch said. "I've seen much scarier things than a few little lights."

They entered the cemetery and walked along the path. Deadman's Hill was a few hundred yards away. The ground was covered with snow now, but it was only a quarter inch deep.

"I was thinking," Barry said. "Those orange lights sound like fireflies to me. Maybe that's all they were."

"Since when do fireflies attack people?" Stan said. "And they don't burn you either. Have you ever caught one? Did it burn your hand?"

"No."

"So that's a pretty dumb idea," Stan said. "These things hurt when they hit me. And fireflies don't come out when it's snowing."

"Maybe they're mutant fireflies," Barry said.

"I told you, these lights form into a giant mass of red fog," Stan said. "Fireflies don't do that. And the little ones are all different colors. Not just orange."

"Maybe they're UFOs," Mitch said. "Tiny flying saucers."

Stan shook his head. "Just shut up," he said. "You'll see when we get there."

But there weren't any lights when they got to Deadman's Hill. No big red glow. No tiny yellow, orange, or blue lights.

"This is the place?" Mitch asked.

"Yeah." Stan looked down the hill at the Chapman gravestone. It was dark. "Follow me," he said.

When he reached the Chapman stone, he brushed some snow from it. "The glow has been right around here the past few nights," he said. "I guess we'll just wait."

They talked softly about other ghosts they'd seen. None of them had seen anything like the flying lights before.

"Ghosts usually have a human shape," Mitch said. "Some of them even talk."

"Maybe they don't like snow," Barry said. "Maybe that's why they aren't out."

Stan brushed some snow from his shoulder. "It was snowing last night," he said. "Not very hard though. But I don't see why snow would bother them."

"Maybe it puts out their lights," Barry said. "Like water puts out a fire."

They waited for about a half hour. By then the snow was a half inch deep.

"My feet are freezing," Barry said. "I don't think we're going to see anything."

"Yeah, let's go," Mitch said. "We'll try again in a couple of days. Let us know if you see anything in the meantime."

Stan walked to the entrance with the other two. Then he decided to take the shortcut back through the cemetery. When Mitch and Barry were out of sight, he took out his notepad.

Stan's Journal: Wednesday, December 13. 9:30 p.m.?

Too cold for the lights? Too snowy? I think it's about 30 degrees. Light wind. Snow is falling pretty hard. Quite peaceful, actually. I love the cemetery at night.

Stan walked back up Deadman's Hill. Still no sign of the lights. He clicked on his flashlight and shined it at the Chapman gravestone. He walked down the hill toward it.

He moved the beam from gravestone to gravestone. William. Eldred. Winnie. Paul. Then his light went out.

What is wrong with this thing? he wondered. He shook the flashlight, but it wouldn't come back on. He clicked it on and off, but it was dead.

Oh well, he thought. *I don't need any light.* He looked up toward the treetops and thought about Paul Chapman. He was the only child from that family who hadn't died in 1918.

Maybe Paul had the flu, too. But he survived. It must have been tough to have all of your brothers and sisters die at once. Stan wished he could talk to Paul Chapman. But he'd been dead for many years now.

Stan had to be home by ten o'clock. He took a final look around, then headed back up the slope. His feet made a shifting sound in the snow as he walked. He was warm. He took off the ski mask and shoved it into his pocket. The mask had blocked some of his view.

As he passed the top of the hill, he noticed that the snow on the ground looked shiny. Had the moon come out? He looked up. The sky was thick with clouds. It was still snowing.

The snow around him turned orange. He didn't have to look. He knew that the orange lights had returned.

Stan started to run. Suddenly, there were orange lights on both sides of him. They were flying right next to him!

"Get lost!" Stan said. Several lights came at him at once. He ducked, but one caught him in the ear. Another landed on his arm. His coat sizzled where it hit. A third one burned through his pants at the knee. Stan leaped from pain and swatted at his leg.

He fell to the ground and orange lights dived at him. They nicked his cheek and the top of his head. He punched at them with both fists.

Where are the yellow ones? Stan thought as he tried to fight. They might be his only hope for rescue.

The lights were stinging all of his exposed skin. A few had burned through his clothing. Stan rolled in the snow, hoping to stomp them out.

Suddenly a bright light shined in his face. The orange lights zoomed away and headed up the hill.

Stan got to his knees. "Who's there?" he said.

"It's me." Amy held the light to her face. "You okay?"

Stan scooped up some snow and rubbed the burned spots on his face with it. "I think so," he said. "They had me though. I couldn't get away."

He looked at his glove. A spot the size of a quarter had been burned through. He poked at the skin underneath. It stung a little, but not too bad.

"How did you find me?" he asked.

"I stopped by your house. Your mom said you were out, so I figured you had to be in the cemetery. Then I heard you yelling."

"Thanks," Stan said. "Good thing you scared them off."

"Just the orange ones, huh?" Amy said.

Stan nodded. "Just the ones that hate me." He smiled. "I've been out here for an hour. There was no sign of them until a minute ago."

"Did you do something to make them mad?" Amy asked.

Stan shook his head. "I don't know. I shined my flashlight on a few of the gravestones. But then my light died."

"Which stones?"

Stan waved his hand toward Deadman's Hill. "On the other side. The Chapmans."

Amy looked stunned. "What was that name?"

"Chapman. There are a whole bunch of them. The kids all died in 1918."

Amy stared at the hill. "That was my mother's name."

"Chapman?"

"Yeah. Before she got married. Those might be her relatives."

"Do you know anything about those kids?" Stan asked.

"No. I've never heard that story." She shined her flashlight beam at the hill. "Can we go see?"

"Not tonight," Stan said. "I've had enough. How about in the morning before school? Sound okay?"

Amy shrugged. "I guess. I'll probably be up all night wondering though." She put a finger to a burned spot near Stan's ear. "That hurt?" she asked.

"Yeah. But not too much." The lights

hadn't done a lot of damage. Not this time anyway.

The big question was why did they want to hurt him? What had he ever done to them? And how much did Amy's arrival in the neighborhood have to do with all this? He'd never seen those lights before she came to town.

Could her Chapman connection have anything to do with it?

"Let's get out of here," Stan said. He looked back at the hill. A few tiny orange lights were floating near the top.

"Keep your flashlight on," he said to Amy. "I don't feel like getting attacked again."

Stan's Journal: Wednesday, December 13. 11:20 p.m.

Those orange lights keep floating around out there. Sometimes they come close to the yard. Other times they stay up on the hill. I'm trying to ignore them.

Amy said she'd ask her mother about the Chapmans.

That was a long, long time ago, but Paul Chapman might have been a great uncle or something. She might know what happened back in 1918. And why those kids never really got to rest.

I have dozens of small burns on my face and neck. There are a few where they burned through my clothes. I thought ghosts were supposed to be icy cold. Not these. That's the strangest thing about them.

Or maybe the strangest thing is that they want to kill me.

Chapter 11:
Chester Burns

Early the next morning, Stan walked through his yard and headed toward Amy's house. He followed the footprints in the snow from the night before.

A quick movement to his left made Stan jump. But it was just a squirrel.

He saw Amy walking toward him, so he waited.

"How are the burns?" Amy asked.

"Okay," Stan said. "You can see the marks, but they don't hurt much."

"The Chapman stones are up there," Stan said, pointing toward Deadman's Hill. "Did you ask your mother about those kids?"

Amy shook her head. "I wanted to read the stones first," she said. "I'll ask her later."

They climbed the hill. Stan could see that the snow around the gravestones was stained orange and yellow. "Look at that," he said.

The stains were small, but clear. "What do you think happened?" Stan asked. "Did some of them die?"

"Maybe they had a fight," Amy said. "Good against evil."

Stan shivered. He stared at the big Chapman stone.

"So these were the kids," Amy said. "Winnie, William, Eldred, and Paul."

"Paul died much later," Stan said. "His stone is newer, see?"

Amy shook her head slowly. "It feels peaceful here," she said. "I'm sure these aren't the bad ghosts."

"Do you think they're the yellow lights?"

Amy nodded. "I'll bet they are." She stepped toward another group of gravestones. "That orange force probably isn't kids."

Stan waved his hand to the side of the hill. "There are more graves from 1918 over there. A lot of them."

"Bad year, huh?" Amy said.

"They all got sick at once."

"So sad," Amy replied. "It was way before my mom was born. But if these Chapmans are from her family, then she might have heard about it."

"Look at those," Stan said, pointing toward a group of gravestones. "See anything strange?"

The stones were very old. The ground below them was clear and dry.

"Wow," Amy said. "Everything else is covered in snow."

Stan held his hand above the dry ground. "It's warm!" he said.

The sun was barely up. The morning was much too cold for any of the snow to have melted. He tested another grave. It was warm, too.

"Look closer," Amy said, putting a finger to the stone. "This looks like blood. Fresh blood."

Stan moved closer to the stone. He touched one of the drops. "It is blood," he said. "At least, I think it is. But it's more orange than red."

Amy read the name on the stone. "Chester Burns. Born 1853. Died 1922."

"So he didn't die of the flu," Stan said.

"No. At least not in 1918," Amy said. She counted the graves that didn't have any snow. "Five of them. And they all died in the early 1920s."

"This is so weird," Stan said.

"I don't get it," Amy said. "These graves are warm. They've been active very recently. Probably last night. I think you might be looking at your enemies right here."

Stan stepped off the grave and onto the snow. He stared at the gravestone of Chester Burns.

"Burns," he said. "How do you like that? His name was Burns and he tried to burn me."

"That's funny," Amy said.

Stan rolled his eyes. "Oh yeah. A big laugh."

"You know what I mean," Amy said. "Odd, not humorous."

"I know what you meant."

"Besides," Amy said, "you don't know if Chester Burns had anything to do with that. He's been dead a long time. We don't know if he's a ghost."

"True," said Stan. "But look at this grave. It's warm. No snow. There are splashes of orange blood on the stone."

"Yeah," Amy said. "I'll bet he was one of the orange lights."

"And the Chapmans are the yellow ones."

"I hope so," Amy said. "I'd like to think that my relatives are trying to protect you. Not kill you."

"Ask your mom what she knows," Stan said. "I'll meet you tonight after dinner."

Stan's Journal: Thursday, December 14. 7:17 a.m.

Lots of clues, but no solution. It seems to me that there is a battle going on in that cemetery. The good force is the yellow lights. The bad force is orange. The other colors seem gentler. They all come together as a red fog sometimes. Maybe they don't have enough ghostly energy to stay apart for long. So they mass into one for protection. Or for community. Or for some other reason that I don't understand.

I may never know the real truth. But I'll keep trying to find out.

Chapter 12:
Let Them Rest

"My ankle still hurts," Jared said as he and Stan left the school that afternoon. "If we were attacked, I'm not sure I could get away."

"They won't attack before sundown," Stan said. "At least, they haven't before. Let's go out there now and snoop around."

Jared agreed. "But not at night," he said. "Trying to run away from ghosts in the dark would not be fun."

All of the snow had melted. They walked slowly, and Jared didn't complain about his ankle. He whistled when he saw the orange splatters on Chester Burns's gravestone. The drops had dried to the color of rust.

"You say these were still wet this morning?" Jared asked.

"Yeah. Wet and orange."

Jared bent down and put his hand over the grave. "And this area was warm?"

"It sure was."

"It isn't now," Jared said. "But I believe you. I talked to Amy at lunch. She told me what happened last night and this morning."

"She did?"

Jared nodded. "I could tell she wasn't lying. She seemed scared."

Stan poked at one of the rust stains. It was dry. "She never seems scared to me," he said. "Did she tell you about the Chapmans?" Stan pointed up the hill to the big Chapman stone.

"A little," Jared said. "Like they might

be her distant cousins or something."

They walked to the Chapman area and took a close look at the stones. "See anything unusual?" Stan asked.

Jared shook his head. In daylight, they didn't appear to be different from the many other gravestones on the hill. All of the stones in this area were quite old. Some were cracked. Many were crooked.

Stan heard a sound behind him. He turned. The old man he'd seen the day before was walking toward them.

"You shouldn't be here," the man said.

"Why not?" Stan asked. He'd visited this cemetery almost every day of his life. No one had ever told him to leave.

"You don't belong here," the man said. He was dressed in the same old-fashioned blue suit. Same black necktie. His gray hair was short and neatly combed, but his suit was ragged and dirty. "You're disturbing the dead."

"How?" Stan asked. "We're not being noisy. We're careful."

The man's face flashed with anger. He pointed a bony finger at Stan. "You run through here at night. Don't deny it. And you shine your light on the graves. Leave these people alone! Let them rest."

That was true. But Stan hadn't started it. He'd only been running because he'd been chased.

"Stay away from here or you'll be sorry," the man said. "You know nothing of the powers within this cemetery. You may think you've seen and felt the anger of the departed, but there's so much more. I'm warning you. You'll be as dead as those beneath this ground if you continue to trespass here."

Stan knew that he wasn't trespassing. This cemetery was owned by the town. He had every right to be here. But the man was very creepy.

"Let's go, Jared," Stan said. He started walking up the hill, away from the man.

Stan looked back when he reached the top of Deadman's Hill. The man was in the same spot, watching them go.

"What a mean guy," Jared said.

"Yeah. He's nuts. How would he know if we were disturbing the dead?"

"Have you ever seen him before?" Jared asked.

"Once." Stan stopped walking. They were out of sight of the man now. "Let's wait a minute," he said. "I want to see where he goes."

Stan dropped to his knees and began crawling back up the hill. "Stay low," he whispered.

"I can't," Jared said. "My ankle. I'll wait here."

Stan crawled to a point where he could see down the hill. The man was gone. The sun was nearly down, so the light had faded.

I should still be able to see him, Stan thought. *Or hear him walking away.*

Stan stood and scanned the cemetery. There was no sign of the man. So he walked back down the hill toward the gravestones.

The snow was all gone, but he could see a trace of footprints in the dry grass. The prints were light orange in color. They led from the Chapman area back to the gravestone of Chester Burns. And that's where they stopped.

"Jared!" Stan called. He waited for Jared to hobble over the hill.

"I think we're on to something," Stan said. He pointed at the orange footprints. "That was Chester Burns we just talked to. Chester Burns the Undead!"

Stan's Journal: Thursday, December 14. 5:35 p.m.

One ghost identified. He even speaks! But who are those other orange lights? How do we stop them?

I'm mad now. One mean ghost can't keep me out of Hilltop Cemetery. I'll be out there tonight. And I'll be ready for a battle.

Chapter 13:
Light and Mirrors

That night, Amy and Stan walked along Washington Street to the Hilltop Cemetery entrance. Stan had made arrangements to meet Mitch and Barry there at nine o'clock.

Jared had sent an e-mail to Stan about items that might help battle a ghost. So Stan had several things in his coat pocket that might be useful.

"My mother said she knew Paul Chapman," Amy said. "He was her grandfather's cousin. Paul died when Mom was a girl, but she said he was nice."

"Did she know about the ones who died of the flu?" Stan asked.

"She said Paul never mentioned them. There were rumors in the family, but Mom didn't know any facts."

"I guess the only fact that matters is that they're your relatives," Stan said. "And maybe they're still with us." He waved toward the graveyard. "Out there."

"I know," Amy said. "It's kind of neat that they're all still together. But I don't like that they're battling those orange ghosts. I want them to be safe."

Stan told her about the man who had confronted him in the cemetery. "I'm sure it was the ghost of Chester Burns," he said. "I think he's the enemy. If we can stop him, your cousins might finally get some peace."

Stan could see Mitch and Barry sitting on a wall by the entrance. Barry stood when he saw them coming.

"Hope tonight isn't another dud," he said. "Like last night."

"I already told you," Stan said. "I got attacked right after you left last night. You saw my burns."

"Maybe those marks are chicken pox!" Barry said with a laugh.

Mitch snorted. "We'll believe it when we see it."

"You sure will," Amy said. "I just hope you don't get so scared you run home to your mothers."

Barry laughed. "Not likely."

They entered the graveyard. "Maybe we should split up," Stan said. "Go in pairs."

"Okay," Mitch said. "What's the plan?"

Stan motioned for everyone to come closer. "Remember what I told you last night?" he said. "The red glow starts by that big gravestone on Deadman's Hill."

Stan poked Barry in the chest. "You and Mitch sneak up to the top of the hill. Stay there and be quiet."

Stan turned to Amy. "We'll circle around like last time," he said. "Through the woods. We'll stay in those bushes at the bottom of the hill."

"And then what?" Barry asked. "You need a better plan than that."

Stan had a few ideas, but he didn't want to share them with Mitch and Barry. "Just be patient," he said. He reached into his pocket and took out a small mirror. "Take this," he said, handing it to Mitch. "Be careful. It's glass. But it might be useful. I have another one."

Mitch and Barry walked away. After they'd gone a few hundred yards, Amy spoke up.

"What's with the mirror?" she asked.

"Ghosts aren't supposed to see

themselves," Stan said. "At least that's what Jared said. It spooks them."

"Why?"

"Sometimes they don't even know that they're dead," Stan said. "It's why they're still wandering around. If they see their reflection it shakes them up. It might even get rid of them for good."

"Oh," Amy said. "What else do you have?"

"Garlic. They hate that. And a small flashlight. My big one still isn't working right. Do you have yours?"

"Yes." Amy took out her light and clicked it on and off.

By the light, Stan could see that Amy looked sad.

"You okay?" Stan asked.

She nodded. "I just feel bad about those Chapman kids. I mean, I assume the yellow lights are them. They seem very playful and happy except when they're fighting the orange ones."

Stan let out a sigh. He felt bad, too. The yellow lights fought the orange ones when they attacked him. They were trying to protect him. They must have known that Stan was harmless. Why didn't the orange ones know that?

"It seems to me that the orange lights are keeping the others from being safe," Amy said.

Stan put his finger to his lips. "Quiet now." They went wide around Deadman's Hill, taking their time. The night was very dark.

Stan rubbed his hands together for warmth. He could see his breath as he and Amy walked.

They settled in the woods at the bottom of the hill. It wasn't long before they saw the lights.

"Orange ones," Amy whispered, pointing. The lights were in the area near

Chester Burns's grave.

"Yellow ones, too," Stan said. There were three of them floating down the hill.

Stan had an idea that he hoped would work. He swept his arm, letting Amy know that they should go. They stepped into the clearing and walked slowly toward the yellow lights. Then they stopped.

The yellow lights circled slowly above Amy and Stan. They were the size of birds, and moved very smoothly.

"Hi," Amy said. "Do you know who I am?"

Suddenly the orange lights sped toward them. The yellow ones flew up the hill and vanished. And the orange ones began attacking. This time they darted at Amy, too.

Stan swung at the lights as he ran toward Burns's grave. All except the biggest one backed away. The big one nicked his ear. Once again, it stung.

"Bring that mirror!" Stan yelled, hoping Mitch and Barry would hear. He reached into his pocket and grabbed his mirror, too. He held it up at the big orange light.

The light moved quickly away, rising above him. Stan could see a reflection in the glass. It was the man he'd spoken to that afternoon.

"Chester Burns!" Stan said. "You leave those kids alone."

The man scowled. Stan looked up. The orange glow was bright and it was swirling. It had no face. But its reflection certainly did!

Mitch and Barry were running down the hill. "Hold up your mirror!" Stan said.

Mitch caught the reflection in the glass.

Amy clicked on her flashlight and shined it at the orange glow. It split into several balls of light. In his mirror, Stan could now see several ghosts. They all looked scared. All except the ghost of Chester Burns.

"Keep the light on him!" Stan shouted. "That's old man Burns."

Burns seemed to be in pain now. The beam from the flashlight was making him scream.

"More light!" Stan said.

Barry turned on a flashlight and focused it on the brightest orange light. Stan watched in his mirror as Burns began sinking to the ground.

The other orange lights had drifted away. They were floating nearby. Stan kept his attention on Burns.

"He's not done yet," Stan said. He could see the orange light and its reflection. The light got brighter. Burns looked even angrier.

"He's gaining strength!" Stan said. "Put more light on him. And get closer with that mirror, Mitch."

The orange glow grew as bright as a flame. It got bigger and began to rise again. Then it tightened into an ember and shot straight toward Stan.

"Duck!" yelled Amy. But it was too late. Stan dropped the mirror. The orange light smacked against his forehead. He fell back and saw stars.

This is it! Stan thought. He covered his head with his arms, waiting for a bigger attack. But all he heard was the ghost of Chester Burns.

"Stop it!" Burns yelled. "Leave us alone!"

"You leave us alone," shouted another voice.

It was Jared!

Stan rolled to his stomach and got up to his knees. He picked up his mirror and directed it at Burns. He could see Jared now, holding a much larger mirror in one hand and a strong flashlight in the other. Burns was caught between the three mirrors and the flashlights. He was quickly fading away.

"Don't let up!" Stan said. He moved closer to what was left of the glow. The others did, too. They surrounded Burns's grave and watched as the dirt turned orange. A mist rose from the ground, then sank slowly into the earth.

Stan handed his mirror to Barry. "Keep that aimed right at the grave," he said. He took out his flashlight and shined it there, too.

Stan looked around. Three flashlights. Three mirrors. Five Zombie Hunters.

"How do we make sure he stays in that grave?" Barry asked.

"These lights will do it," Stan said.

"I mean forever," Barry said. "What happens when we leave?"

Stan knew the answer. He had lots of garlic in his pocket. They would break up the cloves and sprinkle them over the grave. That should do it.

Amy and the Zombie Hunters stood there for a long time, staring at the grave. When Stan looked up, he saw the other orange lights floating above him. There were four of them.

Now what? he wondered.

As he watched, the orange lights turned different colors. One blue, one green, one purple, one red. Maybe they weren't so mean after all. Maybe it was all Burns's doing. He was the one who made them act evil.

"Let me have your mirror," Stan whispered to Jared.

Jared handed him the big mirror.

Stan looked up at the lights. "Don't worry," he said to them. "This won't hurt you." He tilted the mirror so the lights would be reflected. And he saw four smiling faces. They didn't look mean at all.

Up the hill, the big red glow was floating

gently. As the kids watched, three yellow balls of light emerged from the big one. They settled on the small gravestones of the Chapman children.

"Stay here," Stan said, pointing to Jared, Barry, and Mitch. He and Amy walked up the hill toward the yellow lights.

"I'm Amy," she said as they reached the Chapman section. "You're my cousins. My great-grandfather's cousins, I mean."

The lights got a little brighter. Then they floated up and joined the big red glow.

"Amazing," Stan said. "We were right about them. I didn't think we'd ever know."

"Good thing Jared got here," Amy said. "How did he find us?"

"I told him we'd be out here," Stan said. "I guess he couldn't resist. A good Zombie Hunter always looks out for his friends."

"A good cousin does, too," Amy said. "I think we set them free."

Stan went back to the others. He pulled

the garlic from his pocket and handed each of the boys several cloves. "Break these up," he said. "Spread it all over the grave."

"Our hands will stink for days," Barry said.

"It'll keep you safe," Stan said with a grin. "I'll put fresh garlic here every week. That will keep Burns down there where he belongs."

Chapter 14:
The Fifth Zombie Hunter

Stan's Journal: Thursday, December 14. 11:39 p.m.

The yellow lights followed us home. They went back when we reached the edge of the cemetery. I'm pretty sure we'll see them again. And I'm also sure we won't see Chester Burns for a long, long time.

I wonder how long his ghost has been bothering those poor Chapman kids. Ever since he died in 1922? Amy's glad we helped them. I am, too.

Stan looked out his bedroom window. The sky had cleared and the moon was up. He could see a long way into the graveyard. The trees were making long shadows on Deadman's Hill. That was his favorite place. And he knew it was a safe place again.

There were lots of other ghosts out there. Stan knew that most of them were harmless. But every once in a while, a mean one came along.

He sniffed his hands. He'd washed them four times, but they still smelled like garlic. That was okay. It would remind him of his adventure for a few days.

Stan shut off the light and climbed into bed. He was very tired. He closed his eyes but didn't fall asleep right away. He thought about everything that had happened.

Jared had come through. A Zombie Hunter always does. Barry and Mitch had helped a lot, too. They were all right. And Stan had made a new friend. Amy was smart and brave. They had officially invited her to be a Zombie Hunter after they finished with the garlic.

When Stan opened his eyes, he was surprised that the room wasn't quite dark. There was a soft yellow glow coming from outside.

"Good night, Chapmans," Stan whispered.

The glow grew fainter. And then it was gone. The room was pitch-black again.

Stan rolled over and shut his eyes. He had the most peaceful sleep of his life.

Approaching the Undead
Tips from Stan Summer

Step 1: Gather as much information as you can in secret.

Step 2: Move quietly and calmly. Try not to startle the undead by stepping on branches.

Step 3: Check things out in the daylight. Get an idea for your surroundings and look for signs of the undead.

Step 4: Try not to point light directly at the undead. They don't like this and it can cause problems.

Step 5: Bring backup when possible. There is safety in numbers, especially if the undead is angry.

Step 6: Surround the undead on all sides. You will need help for this as well, so choose your backup wisely.

Step 7: Come prepared. There are several things you can use against the undead. Mirrors, lights, and garlic are a few of the things ghosts hate and will avoid.

Ghost Facts
from Stan Summer

#1: Not all ghosts are icy cold. Some can actually burn you!

#2: Mirrors spook ghosts. When they can't see a reflection, it tells them they aren't alive.

#3: Garlic keeps ghosts away.

#4: Not all ghosts have bodies. Some appear as balls of light.

#5: Not all ghosts are angry. Some are playful, others are protective. Be sure to get to know the undead in your area before deciding if it is mean.

#6: Ghosts have good memories.

#7: Ghosts are loyal to their families. Even new generations are treated as family though they've never met.

#8: Graveyards are fun. They are even more fun when the undead are there to play laser tag with!

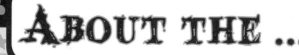

Author

Baron Specter is the pen name of Rich Wallace, who has written many novels for kids and teenagers. His latest books include the Kickers soccer series and the novel *Sports Camp*.

Illustrator

Setch Kneupper has years of experience thinking he saw a ghost, although Graveyard Diaries is the first series of books he's illustrated about the ordeal.